Police Officer

Jillian Jones

Norton in Danger

My alarm clock rang like a police siren. It woke me from a really good dream. Norton and I were being presented with the show jumping cup.

Unfortunately for Jillian Jones, she had knocked the rails on every single jump in the event. Norton, of course, cleared every jump easily.

After all that riding in my dream,
I was hungry. In the kitchen, Dad kissed
me goodbye and left for work. But he
forgot to take his newspaper. I rushed
after him, but he'd already driven away.

Bad news is never good. But when I saw the headline on the back page of the paper, I was shocked. I needed to check on Norton right away.

Just like every other morning, Norton
waited patiently for me at his gate. He
had no idea what danger he might be in.

As a responsible horse owner, it was up to me to tell Norton about the pony kidnappers. Norton listened very carefully to what I had to say.

Norton was so upset he could hardly
eat. I wanted to stay with him, but I had
to hurry. The school bus was coming.

I liked going to school on the school
bus. People on the bus were always
friendly. I'm sure James Gordon didn't
mean to trip me with his huge shoe.

Luckily, I landed on a soft cushion and didn't hurt anything. Unluckily, I missed my chance to wave goodbye to Norton.

Chapter 2

Where is Norton?

At school I sat at my desk, wishing I were back in the paddock with Norton. How could I concentrate on maths when there were pony robbers on the loose?

I couldn't bear to think of it. If those awful robbers took Norton, they might force him to become a getaway horse for their evil gang. It was unthinkable!

Or they might sell him into slavery!
Norton might end up working in the
coal mines.

Or worse! They could sell him to some awful girl. It could even be Jillian Jones! She wouldn't love and care for Norton like I do. She'd drag him off to every show in the district. Of course he'd win, but that doesn't matter.

Then Jillian Jones would take home
the ribbons that should have been mine!

And when she was finished with my
poor pony, she'd toss him outside all
alone like he was an old donkey.

Then some mean person might find him and make him give pony rides at fairs. My noble Norton would have to walk around in circles all day long. Whiny, spoiled little kids would bounce on his back.

Then, when Norton was so tired he couldn't take another step, he'd be put on the merry-go-round. More circles. More howling. More spoiled kids. Oh no! My poor, poor pony!

I drew a picture of Norton in my maths book. He looked terrible. Well, you would too if you'd been through all those awful things. Worrying about Norton was making me feel terrible too.

Mr. Dempsey saw the picture I had drawn in the maths book. He must have thought it was good because he said I had to go and show the headteacher.

But the headteacher didn't like my picture. She gave me detention for scribbling in my book.

But I didn't really care. I just wanted to go home and check on Norton.

✳ Chapter 3 ✳
Searching
For Clues

At last, it was time to go home. The
ride home on the bus seemed to take
forever. *Please, Norton,* I thought. *Please
be waiting for me at the gate.*

I jumped off the bus and ran to
Norton's paddock. The paddock gate was
open. Norton was nowhere to be seen. I
had a sick feeling in my stomach.

I took a deep breath and tried to stay calm. I searched for clues. The robbers might have left something behind.

I checked inside Norton's feed bin. It was empty. *At least Norton hadn't been forced to leave on an empty stomach,* I thought with relief.

A couple of hairs from Norton's mane were caught on the gate. I collected them as evidence. I felt like a detective on TV.

Norton's halter hung on the gate.
There were teeth marks on the leather.
I was pretty sure the marks were from
Norton's teeth, not the robbers. But you
never could tell!

I went into the paddock. All I found
was an empty crisp packet and a few piles
of manure. I was pretty sure the manure
belonged to Norton. But the robbers could
have been eating the crisps.

I took the empty packet.

Mum was picking carrots from the vegetable garden. Norton loves carrots. He would never leave home if he knew Mum was picking carrots. Not unless he had no choice!

"Mum, have you seen Norton?"
I asked.

"No, dear, I thought he was with you," she said.

I took a carrot to show the police.

I found my dad in the garage, fixing his car.

"Dad, have you seen Norton?" I asked.

"No, Molly. Pass me that spanner, will you?" he asked.

Chapter 4

One True Friend

I didn't think the robbers would have
brought Norton into the garage. But I
checked anyway, just in case. All I found
was an old currycomb.

Norton was out in the wide world.
He was alone without his one true friend.
It was time for action. I gathered my
evidence.

I had some of Norton's mane hair and an empty feed bin. I had an empty crisp packet, a carrot, and an old currycomb.

"Hello. Police? There's been a pony-napping. You'd better come quick!" I said.

When the policeman came, I showed him all the evidence. I told him all about the robbers, the coal mine, Jillian Jones, the pony rides, and the merry-go-round.

But the policeman didn't seem to
be listening. He kept asking questions.
"Did you latch the gate? Where have
you looked?"

"I always latch the gate," I said. "And I've looked everywhere."

I took the policeman to the garden. Then the garage. Finally, I took him to see Norton's paddock.

The policeman was wasting time.
Didn't he know that this was a case of
life or death for Norton? The policeman
pointed to hoofprints.

"They must be Norton's," I said wisely.

The hoofprints led away from the paddock, toward the barn. I warned the policeman to be careful. If we went in the barn, we might be ambushed. Bravely, I led the way. And guess what?

There was Norton. Thank goodness he was okay. My clever pony had outsmarted the robbers by hiding in the barn!

"Well, that was a waste of time," said the policeman.

I don't know why the policeman was so angry. There's just no pleasing some people.

After all, I'd found Norton, hadn't I?

Norton was safe from the robbers now.
Safe with me, his one true friend.

✽The End✽

PONY CARE

Keeping a pony safe and happy means paying close attention to the area it lives in.

✳ A stable or barn is a good place to give a pony shelter from the hot sun or cold wind and rain. To make the area comfortable, a stable is usually lined with a bedding of straw or wood shavings.

✳ The stable area should be cleaned out every day. Use a pitchfork to clean up the dirty, wet bedding, and replace it with a fresh layer.

✳ Ponies need plenty of fresh water and food. They drink 30 to 45 litres of water a day and are fed at least twice a day. In warm weather, ponies may be left to get food on their own. They graze on grass in fields. In winter, they are fed hay and grain.

✳ Ponies also need exercise every day. A paddock gives ponies room to run.

The paddock area should have a well-built fence to keep the pony safe. Make sure there are no sagging or broken wires that a pony could become tangled in and injure himself.

Always check that you have closed the gate properly after visiting the paddock. You don't want your pony to make a getaway!

ABOUT THE AUTHOR

While growing up, Bernadette Kelly desperately wanted her own horse. Although she rode other people's horses, she didn't get one of her own until she was a grown-up. Many years later, she is still obsessed with horses. Luckily, she lives in the country where there is plenty of room for her four-legged friends. When she's not writing or working with her horses, Bernadette takes her two children to pony club competitions.

ABOUT THE ILLUSTRATOR

Liz Alger loves horses so much that she left suburbia to live in the rambling outskirts of Melbourne, Australia. Her new home provides plenty of room to indulge in her passion. Her love of animals, horses in particular, shines through in the delightful and humorous illustrations of Norton, the naughty pony, in the *Pony Tales* series.

GLOSSARY

ambushed attacked

currycomb a rubber tool used to remove mud from a horse's coat

detective a person who solves crimes

evidence information and facts that help prove something

halter a set of straps enclosing an animal's head. A rope or strap for leading may be attached to the halter.

paddock a fenced-in area

❋ DISCUSSION QUESTIONS

1. A boy on the bus is mean to Molly. Have you ever been bullied? Discuss your answer.

2. Do you think it's right to use animals for rides? Why or why not?

3. Did you think Norton was stolen? If so, who did you think took him? If not, what did you think happened to him?

WRITING PROMPTS

1. Some people make posters if they lose their pets. Make a poster for missing Norton. Be sure to draw a picture and include a description of the pony.

2. Write your own story about the pony kidnappers. Be sure to include a headline.

3. Who really found Norton? Write a paragraph explaining your answer.

Take Another Ride with Norton

Norton is a naughty pony. Everyone thinks so. Well, everyone except his owner, Molly. She thinks Norton is the most perfect pony in the whole world, no matter what kind of trouble he causes!

Pony Tales

978 1 4062 6634 4

NORTON'S FIRST SHOW
by Bernadette Kelly
Illustrated by Liz Alger

NORTON SAVES THE DAY
by Bernadette Kelly
Illustrated by Liz Alger

978 1 4062 6633 7

NAUGHTY NORTON
by Bernadette Kelly
Illustrated by Liz Alger

978 1 4062 6636 8